To:
Caroline + Cait
Christmas 2014
Love, BABA

To those who believe.

Sourced Media Books
29 Via Regalo
San Clemente, CA 92673
www.sourcedmediabooks.com

ISBN-13: 978-1-937458-56-0

This publication is designed to provide entertainment value and is sold with the understanding that the publisher is not engaged in rendering legal, accounting, or other professional advice of any kind. If legal advice or other expert assistance is required, the services of a competent professional person should be sought.

-From a Declaration of Principles jointly adopted by a
Committee of the American Bar Association and a
Committee of Publishers and Associations

Printed in China

Chloe
The Clumsy Fairy

Katie Watkins

Illustrated by Lester Lee

Sourced Media Books • San Clemente, CA

Summermeadow was buzzing, the sun shining bright.
Seven fairies awoke in a field of pure white.

Chloe stood first and greeted the dawn,
Reglittered her wings, smoothed her hair with a yawn.

"Penelope, Milla," Chloe sang. "Miss Chantelle!"
"Koko and Lola," she called. "Mirabelle!"

"It's time to get up!" Chloe stretched her arms high
And called out, "Good morning," to a bee passing by.

Then Chloe leaned over her white flower bud
And squealed as she slipped and dropped with a *thud*!

"Oh, that's not a good start," Chloe said, hands on hips.
Then she stood with a groan, checked her petals for rips.

"Catastrophically clumsy," she heard Lola say.
"Well, I'd better get going. I've got a big day."

"Dearest Chloe," called Milla, who noticed her scurry.
"Please tell me, why are you in such a big hurry?"

"A dream," Chloe said, in search of her wand.
"Of a lonely girl beyond Dragonfly Pond."

She'd dreamed of Lily, who was feeling just rotten,
For she'd moved across town and by her friends was forgotten.

Not only would no one invite her to play,
But Nick, the class bully, loved to ruin her day.

He laughed when she wore her new yellow blouse.
"Can't see! It's too bright!" Lily shrank like a mouse.

"It's all up to me," Chloe said with a sigh.
"Do you think I can do it?" she asked a bird passing by.

"I drop things. I fall. Can't keep track of my wand,"
(Which, just at that moment, slipped into the pond).

But she fished it out quickly and waved it up high.
"Oh, look! That's the school!" Chloe shook her wand dry.

"Good morning, Lily," Chloe fluttered her wings
As she floated between the slide and the swings.

But Lily didn't see her. Her eyes were cast down,
And she bumped into Chloe, who dropped to the ground!

"Oh, dear!" exclaimed Lily, who knelt in the grass
And, curious, came closer. "Who are you?" she asked.

Chloe just smiled and brushed off her skirt.
"A fairy," she giggled. "One covered in dirt!"

"I've come here to help you!" she waved her wand high.
"Help me? Are you sure?" Lily asked, feeling shy.

Chloe waited and wondered what her first move should be,
When she slipped off the desk and bumped her left knee.

"Some helper I am," she said from below.
But the lunch bell rang. It was time to go.

Since her first day of school, Lily had eaten alone.
"No one here likes me," she said with a moan.

With a shake of her head, Chloe said, "That's not true,"
Then, while dancing atop Lily's milk, dropped her shoe!

"Hi Lily," said Nick, walking by with his tray.
"Nice headband," he smiled. Lily scowled, "Go away!"

Lily picked up her lunch as Nick's mouth opened wide.
"Come on, Chloe," she whispered. "We're going outside."

With her petal skirt fluttering and wand sparkling bright,
Chloe spotted a small group of girls to their right.

"Oh, look Lily, look! Let's invite them to play!"
"I can't. I don't know them," was all she would say.

Then soon, as they walked, they saw Nick coming near.
"Oh, what does he want?" Lily asked, filled with fear.

Chloe stopped mid-twirl, dropped her wand with a clatter.
"Why, Nick needs a friend! Yes, that's what's the matter!"

"I've got an idea!" Chloe blurted out loud.
"Oh, this will be perfect!" she clapped, feeling proud.

Just then, the bell rang. It was now time for art.
Lily found her supplies. Chloe planned out her part.

A wave of her wand and a teensy bump
Was all it took for the paint to dump.

"Oh, no!" Lily gasped, turning bright as a beet.
The paint had spilled all over her feet!

Nick snickered, "Nice work," and he started to clap,
When *his* paint tipped over right into his lap!

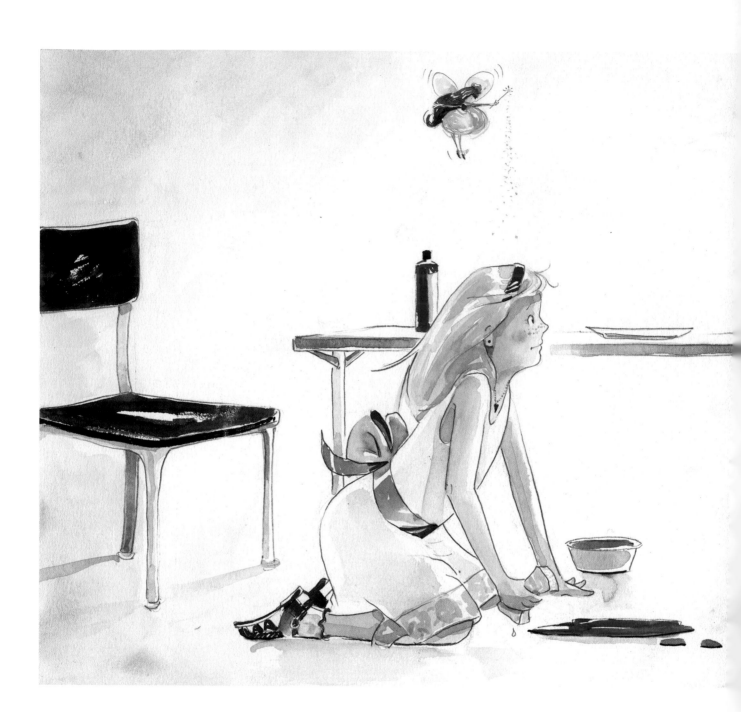

Nick jumped to his feet, his cheeks burning red,
As Chloe dropped fairy dust on Lily's head.

Lily looked up at Nick. "Clumsy day, I guess."
Then she smiled and said, "Should we clean up this mess?"

Nick smiled back, and they cleaned up the floor,
Now friends, at last, and lonely no more.

With fairy dust spilling from a hole in her sack,
Chloe whispered good-bye. "Someday, I'll be back."

"And always remember," she said, looking down,
"You'll find a new friend if you just look around."

"As lonely as lonely might feel to you,
There's always another who needs a friend, too."

She flew out the door toward the meadow beyond
(Then quickly flew back to retrieve her dropped wand).

Back home in the meadow, Chloe twirled with delight
As she told Lily's tale by the fireflies' light.

"I did it!" she said. "Trips, slips, and all!"
Then she laughed with her friends as she started to fall.